THE TREASURE TROOP

Mr. Summerling's Secret Code

by Dori Hillestad Butler

illustrated by Tim Budgen

Penguin Workshop

For Evaline P., who asked me so politely if I'd ever consider writing a *chapter* book about a girl who patches. I'm so glad our paths crossed that day at your school. And thank you (and your parents) for reading this manuscript and helping me get the details right—DHB

For Mum and Dad—TB

PENGUIN WORKSHOP
An Imprint of Penguin Random House LLC, New York

Text copyright © 2021 by Dori Hillestad Butler. Illustrations copyright © 2021 by Penguin Random House LLC. All rights reserved. Published by Penguin Workshop, an imprint of Penguin Random House LLC, New York. PENGUIN and PENGUIN WORKSHOP are trademarks of Penguin Books Ltd, and the W colophon is a registered trademark of Penguin Random House LLC. Printed in the USA.

Visit us online at www.penguinrandomhouse.com.

Library of Congress Cataloging-in-Publication Data is available upon request.

ISBN 9780593094822 (pbk)
ISBN 9780593094839 (hc)

10 9 8 7 6 5 4 3 2 1
10 9 8 7 6 5 4 3 2 1

Marly heard the doorbell ring, but she didn't budge from the couch. Her best friend, Aubrey, had moved to Chicago at the beginning of the summer, so Marly was pretty sure that whoever was at the door wasn't here to see her. And she didn't want to pause the book she was listening to. Not when she was so close to finding out the truth about Sam Westing.

"Can you get that, honey?" Mom called from the kitchen island.

Marly's mom was baking bread for the food pantry. She always did that on the third Saturday of the month. Sometimes Marly helped, but she didn't feel like helping today.

She didn't feel like answering the door, either. She turned up the volume on her audiobook and pretended she couldn't hear her mom.

The doorbell rang again.

"Please, Marly. My hands are covered in dough." Mom held up her hands.

Marly sighed. Dad was out grocery shopping. Nick and Noah were at the pool. So she paused her book and dragged herself to the door.

"It's probably Ellen." Mom walked behind Marly, kneading a ball of dough between her hands. "She said she was going to drop off some work for me today." Marly's mom was an accountant and Ellen was her boss.

Marly peered out the narrow window

beside the door and saw a curly-haired man standing on the porch. He wore a blue shirt and khaki pants, and he held a white envelope in his hands.

"It's not Ellen," Marly told her mom.

"No? Then who is it?" Mom went to the window.

Marly shrugged and opened the door. The man on the porch did a double-take when he saw her, then quickly turned his attention to Mom. "Marly Deaver?" he asked.

"No, this is Marly." Mom tilted her head.

"Oh." The man blinked in surprise. "Well, this envelope is for her," he said, as though Marly wasn't standing right there. Marly was used to that. Grown-ups didn't like to make eye contact with kids who wore eye patches.

Mom didn't have a free hand to take the envelope, so the man thrust it toward Marly. She grabbed it, and the man hurried away.

"What is this?" Marly asked, turning the envelope over. There was no return address or stamp. Just her name typed in all capital letters: MARLENA MARIE DEAVER.

"Excuse me?" Mom called to the man. "What's this about?"

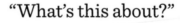

He didn't answer. Without even looking back, the man got into the red car he'd left running in the street and drove away.

Marly tore open the envelope and pulled out

a single, typed sheet of paper. It looked like the sort of letter you'd send to a grown-up, not an almost nine-year-old. Marly read the letter out loud while her mom looked over her shoulder:

Dear Ms. Deaver,

Your presence is requested at the office of Ms. Stella Lovelace, 120 Downtown Plaza, 10:00 a.m. on Monday, July 24, for the reading of Mr. Harry Summerling's will. Please let me know if you cannot attend.

Sincerely,

Stella Lovelace
Attorney-at-Law

"Huh," Mom said. "I didn't know Mr. Summerling passed away."

"What?" Marly said, shocked. "Passed away" was what grown-ups said when they meant "died." "How do you know he . . . passed

5

away?" Mr. Summerling was their next-door neighbor. He was old, but not *that* old.

Everyone in Sandford knew Mr. Summerling because he walked around town with a metal detector. He was always on the hunt for buried treasure. He was also the janitor at the library, but last year he quit his job so he could spend even more time treasure hunting. No one knew whether he ever found any. If you asked him about it, he would gaze thoughtfully into the distance and say something like "Not all treasure is silver and gold."

"If an attorney is reading his will, he must've passed away," Mom said. "That's too bad. He was a nice man. Quirky, but nice."

BEEP BEEP!

"Yeah," Marly said. She didn't know what else to say. No one she knew had ever died before.

She glanced over at the house next door. She couldn't see much of it because of the tall hedge that seperated the two yards. A faded yellow tower stood out above the greenery. The tower looked quiet without Mr. Summerling. Maybe even a little sad.

"If this Ms. Lovelace wants you to be there

when she reads Mr. Summerling's will, he must've left you something," Mom said.

"Me?" Marly perked up. "What would he leave me?"

"That's a good question," Mom said.

"I don't get it," Nick said at dinner. "Why would Mr. Summerling leave something in his will for Marly, but not the rest of us?"

"Yeah," Noah said, passing the pasta to Dad. "That's hardly fair."

Nick and Noah were twins, but you couldn't tell by looking at them. Nick had brown hair like Mom and Noah had blonde hair like Marly and Dad. The twins were four years older than Marly and going into eighth grade.

"He must've liked me better than he liked you," Marly said with a shrug. It wasn't often

she got something that her brothers didn't.

But inside, she couldn't stop wondering what Mr. Summerling had left her. Was it money? Was it buried treasure? And why in the world would he leave her anything at all?

Sure, he was nice. He bought candy and wrapping paper from her when she sold it for school. Sometimes he paid her to sweep his front walk. Once he even gave her one of his old metal detectors when he cleaned out his garage. But he was next-door-neighbor nice, not give-you-something-when-I-die nice.

"Where's your patch?" Mom interrupted Marly's thoughts.

"It was hot, so I took it off."

"Go put it back on, please," Dad said.

"You need to wear it, honey," Mom added. "At least until you see the eye doctor next month."

Marly groaned. There was no point in arguing, so she got up and dragged herself to her room. She was so tired of patching. So tired! Most kids who patched only had to do it for a few months in kindergarten and then they were done. Marly had been patching off and on since she was three years old. And unlike other kids, she had to wear her patch *all day*. It wouldn't be so bad if the patch covered her bad eye. But the whole point of wearing it was to train her bad eye to work like her good eye, which meant covering her *good* eye.

There were two patches on her dresser. She had worn the smiley-face one earlier in the day, so Marly grabbed the pink flower  one instead. Carefully, she threaded it onto the temple of her glasses until it covered her right lens. Then she put her glasses on and everything across the room went blurry.

"Does Marly have to share whatever Mr. Summerling left her with the whole family?" Noah asked their parents when Marly returned to the table.

Mom smiled. "Whatever it is, I can't imagine it's all that valuable."

"It could be," Marly spoke up.

11

"Mr. Summerling was always searching for treasure." Nick stood up and helped himself to another slice of garlic bread. "What if he found some?"

"Yeah, maybe he's got a secret vault at the bank where he stores it all," Noah added.

"Does he?" Nick asked their dad.

Dad would know. He was a banker.

"The Sandford Savings and Loan doesn't have any secret vaults," Dad said, wiping his chin with his napkin. "Only safe-deposit boxes. And if Mr. Summerling had a safe-deposit box or a lot of money, I wouldn't be allowed to tell you. But ..." He winked at Marly. "I wouldn't get too excited if I were you. Whatever he left you is probably more likely to be 'interesting' than valuable."

Marly knew her parents were probably right. But what if they were wrong?

After dinner, she emailed Aubrey:

From: Marly Deaver
To: Aubrey Etoh
Subject: News!

Hi Aubrey,

Remember my neighbor, Mr. Summerling? The guy with the metal detector who searches for buried treasure? Well, you won't believe this, but he died and actually left me something in his will. I don't know what it is yet. I'll find out on Monday. Maybe it's money I could use to buy a plane ticket to come visit you! Wouldn't that be great? Write back soon!

Best Friends Forever,

Marly

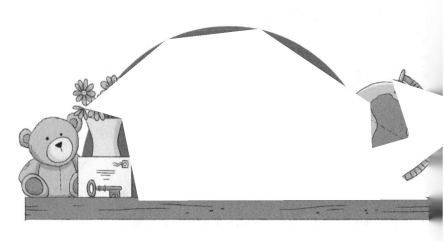

Ms. Lovelace's office was located in a small brick building across the street from the bank where Marly's dad worked.

Marly and her mom walked in and spotted a lady at a desk behind the counter. "Come in, come in," she said. The lady was older than Marly's mom, but not as old as Mr. Summerling. "You must be the Deavers." Like everyone else, she glanced at Marly's eye patch, then quickly looked away.

"Yes," Mom said, checking her watch. They

were a few minutes late.

"Everyone else is already here. I'll take you back to the conference room." The lady led Marly and her mom down the hall.

There were windows looking in to the conference room. Marly was surprised to see two kids she knew from school sitting at a long table in there. Isla Thomson and Sai Gupta. She didn't know either of them very well. But she recognized the back of Isla's head. Isla had long dark hair and she always wore headbands with cat ears. Today's was pink. And everyone knew Sai because he always brought popsicles for the school on field day.

It looked like Isla was here with her mom, who held a sleeping baby in her arms. Sai was here with his dad.

There was another man sitting by himself across from Sai and his dad. He was all dressed up in a dark suit and tie. His thumbs tapped busily on the phone in his hands.

"Welcome!" The lady at the head of the table came to greet Marly and her mom, and everyone turned toward them. Isla and Sai seemed as surprised to see Marly as she was to see them.

"You must be Mrs. Deaver and Marly," the lady went on. "I'm Stella Lovelace, Harry Summerling's attorney." She shook Mom's hand first, then Marly's.

"Please have a seat over there." Ms. Lovelace gestured toward two empty chairs beside the man in the suit. He didn't even glance up from his phone when Marly sat down beside him.

Ms. Lovelace closed the door, then took her seat at the head of the table. "Now that we're all here—" she began.

"Excuse me." Isla's mom gently rocked her baby. "When did Harry Summerling pass away? I never saw an obituary in the newspaper."

"And how did he die?" Sai asked. His dad nudged him and shook his head. Embarrassed, Sai slid down in his chair.

Too bad, because Marly was wondering the same thing. She also wondered how Isla and Sai knew Mr. Summerling. Had he left *them* something in his will, too?

"It's okay," Ms. Lovelace said kindly. "The report from the coast guard says he drowned. He was in a small boat somewhere off the coast of Washington State when a storm came up. The boat was found, but he wasn't in it."

Marly's mom put her hand to her mouth. "That's terrible."

"What was he doing out there?" Isla's mom asked.

The man beside Marly finally put down his phone. "What do you think he was doing?" he said rudely. "He was searching for buried treasure. It's all he ever did."

"Does everyone know Jay Summerling,

Harry's son?" Ms. Lovelace asked.

Marly had lived next door to Mr. Summerling her whole life, but she never knew he had a son. Mr. Summerling's son was about Marly's mom's age.

"We are so sorry for your loss," Sai's dad said, offering a hand to shake.

Jay didn't take it. "Can we get on with this, please?" he said. "I have someplace to be at noon."

Ms. Lovelace winced. "Of course," she said. She opened the folder in front of her and took out a large brown envelope. There were several white envelopes in the folder behind it. She sliced into the brown envelope with a fancy gold letter opener and pulled out a single sheet of paper.

"This is Harry's will," she said, unfolding it. "It's a letter. I'll read it out loud." She cleared her throat. "'If you're hearing this letter, then I am missing, dead, or perhaps I've been abducted by aliens.'" Jay snorted at that. "'And it's time to give away some of my earthly possessions—'"

"*Some* of his possessions?" Jay asked.

"That's what it says," Ms. Lovelace said. "I'm reading this for the first time myself, sir. Shall I continue?"

Jay motioned for her to keep going.

"'To my son, Jay,'" Ms. Lovelace read. "Oh, dear." She paused. "It says, 'I leave ... nothing.'"

"Here we go," Jay muttered.

"'You have been a terrible disappointment to me, son,'" Ms. Lovelace read as the parents shifted uncomfortably in their seats. "'You don't call. You don't visit. And you don't take my treasure hunting seriously. So why should you reap the reward? You don't deserve a share of my treasure—'"

"What treasure?" Jay scoffed. "He never found any treasure."

Ms. Lovelace seemed to be holding back a smile as she continued reading. "'Oh yes, son. There *is* treasure. And I, Harry P. Summerling, being of sound mind and body, will that treasure to Ms. Marly Deaver, Mr. Sai Gupta, and Ms. Isla Thomson—'"

"Wait, what?" Sai said, sitting up a little straighter.

Marly's mouth fell open. "For real?"

"'*If* they can find it,'" Ms. Lovelace continued. "'I have created a series of puzzles for the

three of them to solve. They must work together on each one. When they reach the end of the treasure hunt, anything they find is to be split evenly between them. Stella, please give them the envelope marked #2. Good luck! Sincerely yours, Harry P. Summerling.'"

Marly, Isla, and Sai gaped at each other.

Jay scowled. "That's it? That's all it says?" he asked.

"That's all it says." Ms. Lovelace set the letter on the table.

"I don't understand," Sai's dad said.

Marly's mom was equally confused. "So, there's some sort of treasure," she said. "We don't know what it is, but for some reason, Harry Summerling has hidden it. And if our kids can find it, it belongs to *them*?"

"Yes. That is correct," Ms. Lovelace said.

"But . . . why?" Isla's mom asked. "Why would Mr. Summerling leave treasure to three children he's not even related to?"

"He had his reasons," Ms. Lovelace said mysteriously.

"This is ridiculous," Jay said with a short laugh. "There's no treasure. Now, what about the house? I assume Dad left that to me?"

"I don't know," Ms. Lovelace said, turning the paper over. "This letter doesn't say anything about the house."

"Well, read the other letters." Jay gestured toward the folder in front of Ms. Lovelace.

"I'm sorry. I can't." Ms. Lovelace closed the folder. "Not today. Harry left specific instructions for when each one is to be opened. And by whom. This was the only letter I was supposed to read today."

Jay shoved his chair back from the table. "Well, we'll see what *my* attorney has to say about this," he grumbled. "There is no treasure! I hope you all know that." With that, he stormed out of the room, banging the blinds against the window on his way out.

The baby startled awake. He looked around and started to whimper. Isla's mom put him to her shoulder and rubbed his back.

"So, *is* there a treasure?" Sai asked Ms. Lovelace in a small voice.

"And if there is, is it really ours?" Marly asked.

"Honestly, I don't know what you'll find at the end of this little treasure hunt," Ms. Lovelace said. "But whatever it is, yes, it's yours. Harry was very clear about that."

Marly trembled with nerves and excitement. She would have to go on a treasure hunt with two kids she hardly knew. And share the treasure with them. But when it was all over, hopefully her portion would be enough to buy a plane ticket to Chicago.

Chapter 3

THE FIRST PUZZLE

Ms. Lovelace pulled a white envelope from her folder. "This envelope contains your first clue," she said, holding it up. "Who wants to open it?"

"I do," Marly said at the same time Sai said, "Me!"

"You're closest. Here you go," Ms. Lovelace said, handing Marly the envelope along with the gold letter opener.

Marly slit the envelope open and pulled out a sheet of paper. There were a bunch of holes in it, like maybe Mr. Summerling had used it to test his hole puncher. At the top of the paper was an ink drawing of a man who looked a lot like Marly's neighbor sitting at a desk, and the words *From the Desk of Harry P. Summerling.* Below that, just above the holes, was a message:

"What does it say?" Sai wiggled in his seat.

"I don't know. It's some kind of code."

Marly moved her patch so she could see it more clearly with both eyes. But that didn't help.

Sai hopped down from his chair and came around to Marly's side of the table. "Weird," he said. He was short, so he had to stand on his tiptoes to see over her shoulder.

"Can I please see the paper?" Isla asked.

Marly slid it across the table. The parents all leaned over to get a closer look. And Sai scurried over to Isla's side of the table.

"Can you read it?" Marly asked Isla.

"Not yet," she said, twisting her long hair around her finger.

"I hate to break this up." Ms. Lovelace rose to her feet. "But my next client will be here soon."

"What?" Sai cried. "You're kicking us out? Before we crack the code?"

"I have to get back to the store anyway." Sai's dad rested a hand on Sai's shoulder. "And you have to practice piano and do your homework for summer school."

Sai wrinkled his nose.

"We should go, too. Liam will need to be fed soon," Isla's mom said.

"If everyone's leaving now, when are we going to do the treasure hunt?" Marly asked. The parents exchanged looks. Marly knew that look. And she didn't like it. "You *are* going to let us do it, aren't you?" she asked.

"I don't know, honey," Marly's mom said.

"I don't know, either," Isla's mom said. "I

hate to put our children in the middle of a family feud."

"This isn't a feud. This is what Harry wanted," Ms. Lovelace assured them. "Now, please. Why don't you all exchange contact information so you can figure out when and where your children can get together."

The parents all talked to each other with their eyes again. Finally, Sai's dad said, "I suppose we could let the kids work the puzzles. When they complete the last one and we know what the treasure is, *then* we can discuss whether or not they should keep it."

"I *am* curious what the treasure might be," Isla's mom admitted.

"Isla and Sai are welcome to come to our house," Marly's mom said. "I work from home, so I'll be around. How's two o'clock this afternoon?"

Marly, Isla, and Sai all grinned at each other. While the parents entered each other's information into their phones, Isla folded up the letter with the code and handed it to Marly. "You should take this since we're meeting at your house."

"But remember, you can't start on the code without us!" Sai said.

Marly was dying to start on the code, but she knew that wouldn't be fair. So after lunch, she distracted herself by checking for messages on the iPad. Unfortunately, Aubrey hadn't written back yet.

Marly sighed and emailed Aubrey again:

From: Marly Deaver
To: Aubrey Etoh
Subject: Mr. Summerling's will
Hi Aubrey,
Do you want to know what Mr. Summerling

left me in his will? So do I! A lady read a letter he wrote that said he was leaving treasure to me and Isla Thomson and Sai Gupta. Can you believe that? But we have to solve some puzzles to find it. We don't even know what the treasure is or why he left it for us. I have a feeling Isla might be good at puzzles, but I don't know about Sai. I wish I was doing this with you instead of them. Please write soon!
Best Friends Forever,
Marly

When she finished, it was almost two o'clock. Marly grabbed the paper with the code and went outside to wait for Isla and Sai. Isla was already walking up the front steps.

"Oh. Hi," Marly said.

"Hi," Isla replied.

Marly led Isla to the chairs on the front porch. Neither of them seemed to know what to say next.

That was never a problem with Aubrey. She and Aubrey never ran out of things to talk about. If they did, they played "let's pretend we're . . ."

Marly thought about saying to Isla, *Let's pretend we're movie stars and we're in a restaurant where everyone knows us.* But she was afraid Isla wouldn't know what to do. Or she'd think it was stupid. So instead Marly said, "Do you live close by?"

"Two streets over," Isla said.

"That's pretty close," Marly said.

"Yeah," Isla agreed.

Then: silence.

A few minutes later, a car slowed down in front of Marly's house. The back door opened, and Sai flew out of the car.

Finally, Marly thought. Now she could stop worrying about what to talk about and concentrate on the treasure hunt.

"I'll come back at five o'clock," Sai's mom

called from the car. Sai waved to his mom as he ran up the walk.

"Hey!" he said. "How cool is this? A treasure hunt just for us!"

"Pretty cool," Marly agreed.

Sai boosted himself up onto the porch railing and dangled his feet. "So, how do you guys know Mr. Summerling?"

"He lives—I mean, *lived* right over there." Marly waved in the direction of Mr. Summerling's house.

"Oh, of course," Isla said knowingly. "You live on Forest Street and so did he."

"Yes," Marly said. And there really was a forest behind their houses. But you couldn't get to it because of the tall fences at the back of their yards. "Wait, how did you know Mr. Summerling lived on Forest Street?"

"He was my senior buddy in second grade," Isla said. "We wrote letters back and forth. We still do. Well, we did." She suddenly looked sad. Like maybe she just realized they wouldn't be doing that anymore.

"I had Mr. Hale for second grade, too, but I don't write to my senior buddy anymore. I don't even remember his name," Sai said.

Marly never had a senior buddy when she was in second grade. Mrs. Henry's class didn't do senior buddies.

"How do you know Mr. Summerling?" Marly asked Sai.

"He used to come into my parents' store for

a newspaper and a pint of ice cream. We sell bear tracks, which is his favorite kind," Sai said. "Sometimes he played Monopoly with me when he came in."

"Oh, I love Monopoly!" Marly said. But she didn't get to play very often. Aubrey preferred dress-up and pretend games to board games, and Marly's brothers thought Monopoly was boring.

"We should get to work," Isla said.

"Right," Marly said. Sai hopped down from the railing, and Isla pulled her chair closer. Carefully, Marly unfolded the paper with the first clue:

DIFN HET EASRB NFID
ETH EXNT UCLE

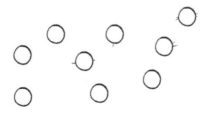

"Why are there so many holes in the paper?" Sai picked it up and looked through one of the holes.

Marly grabbed the paper back. "I don't think we need to worry about the holes. Let's figure out the words."

"Diffin het ease-erb—" Sai tried to read the words out loud. "It's like a foreign language."

"No, it's not!" Isla said, jumping up. Her cat ears slipped back a little on her head and she readjusted them. "Does anyone have a pencil?"

"I'll go get one," Marly said. She handed the paper to Isla, then ran inside to search for a pencil. She found one in the kitchen junk drawer.

"They're scrambled words," Isla said when Marly returned. "If you rearrange the letters, H-E-T and E-T-H both spell THE."

Marly sat down next to Isla and studied the paper. "Hey, you're right!"

Isla laid the paper on her leg and carefully wrote *THE* below the *HET* and the *ETH*.

"Blank THE blank blank THE blank blank," Sai said. "We're going to solve this in no time!" He rubbed his hands together.

"*D-I-F-N* could be *FIND*," Marly said.

"So FIND THE . . . BEARS," Isla said, pointing at the *EASRB*.

"*N-F-I-D* also spells *FIND*." Sai pointed.

"FIND THE BEARS, FIND THE NEXT CLUE," they all said together.

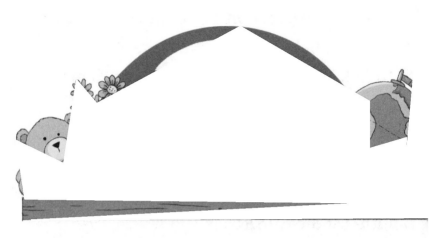

"Bears . . . ?" Sai said, slowly. "We don't have any bears in this town. We don't even have a zoo here."

"I don't think Mr. Summerling wants us to find real, live bears," Marly said. "What other kind of bears could he be talking about?"

"Maybe teddy bears," Sai said. "Do either of you have a teddy bear?"

"My little brothers each have one," Isla said.

Marly rubbed her eye behind her glasses. "You have another brother? Besides the one we saw at Ms. Lovelace's office?"

"Uh-huh." Isla flipped her hair over her shoulder. "That was Liam. He's only three weeks old. Gavin is my other brother. He's five. My sister, Chloe, was babysitting him this morning. Do you have brothers and sisters?"

"Two brothers," Marly said. "Nick and Noah. They're twins. And they're thirteen."

"Lucky! I'm an only child," Sai said. He turned to Isla. "Should we go over to your house and check out your brothers' teddy bears?"

"We could, but I don't think we'll find any clues there," Isla said. "Mr. Summerling never even met my little brothers, so how could he have put a clue in their teddy bears?"

Marly sighed.

"Do you have some more paper?" Isla asked. "Sometimes I think better when I can draw."

"I think better when I walk or run around," Sai said. He started pacing back and forth on the Deavers' porch.

"I'll go see what I can find," Marly said. She went back inside her house and up to her room. Her school backpack was right where she'd left it on her last day of third grade. She grabbed her green science notebook and hurried outside.

At first, she didn't see Isla or Sai. Had they left? Then she saw them on the porch swing. They had their backs to her and they were up on their knees, craning their necks like they were trying to see into Mr. Summerling's yard.

"What are you doing?" Marly asked.

"We were thinking we should walk around Mr. Summerling's house to see if there are any bears in his yard," Sai said, still facing next door.

Isla turned around. "*Sai* was thinking we should do that," she said. "*I* think that would be trespassing."

"Not if we just walk around the house. Right, Marly?" Sai asked. "Does anyone even live there right now?"

"I don't know. I don't think so," Marly replied. Still, she wasn't sure she wanted to walk around his yard, either. Somehow that felt wrong.

Isla walked over to Marly. "Can I draw in that?" She gestured toward the notebook.

"Sure." Marly handed it to her.

Isla sat down on the chair and started drawing. Sai swung back and forth on the porch swing, going higher and higher with each swing. Marly wasn't sure what to do, so she went to see what Isla was drawing.

"Wow, you're good," Marly said. Isla had already drawn several bears. A big one. A little one. A fat one. A skinny one. A funny one. A serious one.

Sai jumped off the swing and came to look. "Yeah, *really* good," he said.

Isla blushed. "Thanks, but I don't think it's helping."

Marly glanced over at the thick hedge that separated her yard from Mr. Summerling's. "I suppose we *could* go walk around next door," she said. It's not like they had any better ideas. And maybe they would find something.

"All right," Isla agreed. Though Marly could tell she still wasn't thrilled with the idea.

But Sai was. "Let's go," he said, leaping down Marly's stairs.

Isla slipped the pencil and paper with the code inside Marly's notebook and they all trooped next door. A tall wrought-iron fence lined the sidewalk in front of Mr. Summerling's house. There was a gate that opened to the front walk, but the gate was padlocked shut.

"That's weird," Marly said. She didn't remember there ever being a padlock on this gate before.

Sai pulled on it. It didn't budge. "We could climb the fence," he suggested.

"No," Marly and Isla said at the same time.

"That would *definitely* be trespassing," Isla said.

"Plus, this would be a hard fence to climb," Marly said. The bars were narrow and tall and there were spiky posts at the top.

"Fine. What do you two think we should do next?" Sai crossed his arms.

They peered through the bars. Paint was peeling on Mr. Summerling's house and there was junk on the porch and scattered all around the yard. Old appliances, bowls, bottles, containers full of scrap metal. There

was also a big oak tree and several scraggly patches of daisies. The surrounding weeds were almost as tall as the flowers.

"See any bears?" Isla asked.

"Nope," Marly said. "No bears. No bear tracks. No—"

"Aha! That's it!" Sai raised his finger in the air.

"That's what?" Marly squinted at him.

"Bear tracks ice cream," Sai said.

44

"Huh?" Isla said.

"Bear tracks ice cream," Sai said again. He started pacing back and forth. "I told you. We sell it at our store. It was Mr. Summerling's favorite kind. And guess what? There are bears on the carton!"

Isla and Marly looked at each other, then at Sai.

Marly grinned. "Let's go check it out."

Chapter 5

Sai's family's store was only four blocks from Marly's house, so all the parents gave permission for Sai, Marly, and Isla to walk there together.

"What do you think we're going to find at the end of this treasure hunt?" Sai asked along the way.

"I don't know. Money?" Marly said.

"Yeah, but how much?" Sai asked.

Marly shrugged. *Hopefully enough to buy a plane ticket to Chicago,* she thought. "What are you going to do with your share of the treasure?" she asked the others.

"Buy a trampoline," Sai said. "But first I'd have to buy my family a house with a yard so I'd have someplace to put my new trampoline."

"I wish I could buy my family a new house, too," Isla said. "One with my own room and a lock, so I could keep my brothers and sister out of my stuff."

Sai turned to Marly. "I bet I know what you're going to spend your share on. A new eye so you don't have to keep wearing that patch."

Isla gasped. "Rude!"

But Marly wasn't offended. "I don't need a new eye," she said. Was that even a thing? An eye transplant? "I need to fix the one I have. That's why I'm wearing this patch."

"What's wrong with your eye anyway?" Sai asked.

"I have amblyopia," Marly said.

Isla blinked in surprise. "I had that!"

"Really?" Marly said. "You had a lazy eye?" She remembered another girl at school who patched a long time ago, but she didn't remember that that girl was Isla. It must've been before she started wearing cat ears.

Isla nodded. "I only had to wear a patch for a few months when I was in kindergarten," she said. "That's why I thought you probably had something different."

"No, I have amblyopia," Marly said. "The eye doctor says I can finally stop patching when I turn nine."

"You're not nine yet?" Sai asked as they walked past a building with four or five shops in it. "Aren't you going into fourth grade?"

"Yes," Marly said, slightly annoyed. "I'll be nine next month."

And it didn't seem like her eye was getting any better. The eye doctor said it wouldn't do any good to keep patching after Marly turned

nine, but she never said what they'd do if Marly's eye wasn't better. Marly didn't even want to think about that.

"Is that your parents' store?" Isla pointed at a tan convenience store across the street. A flashing sign in the window read Rise and Shine.

"Yup," Sai said. "Let's go find the bear tracks!" He looked both ways, then darted across the street.

Marly felt grateful for the change of subject as she and Isla followed Sai. She noticed an old phone booth out by a dumpster at the edge of the parking lot, and a small house that

was connected to the back of the store.

"Is that your house?" Marly asked Sai.

"Yeah," Sai said. He seemed a little embarrassed, but Marly wasn't sure why. She thought it would be fun to live behind a store.

Bells jingled as Sai opened the door to the store. "Hi, Dad," he said.

Sai's dad looked up from the crossword puzzle he was working on at the counter. "Well, if it isn't the treasure hunters!" he said warmly. "How's it going?"

"Fine." Sai led Marly and Isla to a row of

freezers at the back of the store. He opened one of the doors and pulled out a carton of bear tracks ice cream. His face fell. "It's sealed."

"Of course it's sealed," Sai's dad said as he came up behind them.

"Are they all sealed?" Sai put the carton back and checked the other cartons in the freezer.

"I hope so," Sai's dad said. "We can't sell them if they're not. What are you looking for?"

"Our next clue," Sai said. "I thought maybe Mr. Summerling put it in a carton of bear tracks ice cream."

Isla showed Sai's dad the puzzle they'd solved.

FIND THE BEARS, FIND THE NEXT CLUE

The bells on the door jingled again and two boys with skateboards walked in.

"I don't think these are the bears you're looking for," Sai's dad said. Then he went to see if the skateboarders needed any help.

Marly reached for another carton of ice cream. "Maybe there's a clue on the outside of the carton," she said, turning it all around. But if there was, she didn't see it. All she saw was a picture of two bears enjoying a bowl of ice cream on the front of the carton. And a lot of boring nutrition information on the back.

"We're right back where we started," Sai grumbled.

"Well, where else can we find bears?" Isla asked.

Marly put the carton back in the freezer. "The only other bears I can think of are Goldilocks and the three bears."

"That's just a story," Sai said.

"There are a lot of bears in stories," Isla said, twirling her hair. "There's *Brown Bear, Brown Bear* and *Little Bear* and *Corduroy*. My brother checks those books out from the library all the time."

"And Mr. Summerling used to work at the library," Marly said with growing enthusiasm. "Maybe we should go to the library and read some bear books. Maybe that'll give us some new ideas."

"Maybe," Isla said. "But"—she checked her watch—"we can't go today. My mom's picking me up soon."

"We could meet there tomorrow morning," Sai said. "Anyone know what time it opens?"

"Ten o'clock," Marly and Isla said at the same time. The only other person Marly did that with was Aubrey. She smiled at Isla and Isla smiled back.

"Okay. I'll meet you at the library tomorrow at ten o'clock," Sai said.

That night Marly emailed Aubrey again.

From: Marly Deaver
To: Aubrey Etoh
Subject: Guess what!

Hi Aubrey,

Isla, Sai, and I solved the first puzzle! But we're stuck on the second puzzle. Did you know Sai lives behind a little store? And Isla is really good at drawing. If I can't hang out with you, they aren't so bad to hang out with. Hey, I have an idea! Let's pretend we're . . . best friends who got separated by a thousand miles because one of them moved away. How do they stay friends? They email each other! PLEASE WRITE SOON!!!!!

Your best friend forever who misses you a lot,

Marly

The next morning, Marly's mom drove her and Isla to the library.

"Do you see Sai?" Marly asked, shouldering her tote bag. Their notebook was inside the tote bag.

"Not yet," Isla replied. Today's cat ears were black with red polka dots.

"I'm going inside," Mom said. "Come find me by the magazines when you're finished."

Marly and Isla sat down on a bench to wait for Sai.

"Look." Isla pointed at the wood sculpture next to one of the other benches. It was a life-size mother bear and baby bear. From the *Little Bear* books. The mother bear was reading to baby bear. Marly slid her patch onto the temple of her glasses so she could see better. "Hey, maybe *those* are the bears we're supposed to find," she said, hopping to her feet. "Let's go see."

Isla grabbed Marly's arm. "We should wait for Sai."

Marly sat back down. Isla was right.

A few minutes later, Sai's mom pulled into the library parking lot and Sai jumped out of the car. Marly and Isla ran to meet him.

Sai looked at Marly. "Aren't you supposed to wear your eye patch over your eye?"

Marly scowled. "I'm taking a break. Look over there." She pointed to the wooden sculpture.

"Bears!" Sai exclaimed. "That's got to be where our next clue is, right?"

They raced to the sculpture, then slowly walked around it, examining it from all angles.

"I don't see anything," Sai said after a few seconds.

Isla ran her hand all around the bears and under the book in the mother bear's hand. "It's solid wood. There's no place to hide a clue."

"Another dead end," Marly said, disappointed.

Sai stood on his tiptoes so he could see the pages of the book in the mother bear's hand.

"There are words carved into these pages. Maybe there's a clue in the words?"

"I doubt it. That's just a page from one of the *Little Bear* books," Isla said.

"Wait a minute," Marly said, staring at the wooden page. It was about the size of the paper their code had been written on. She reached into her tote bag and pulled out their notebook. The paper they'd decoded was still in the back pocket.

"What are you doing?" Isla asked.

"I saw this in a movie once." Marly

unfolded the paper and laid it over the open pages of the wooden book. Then she grinned. "Looks like there's more to the holes in this paper than we first thought." She stepped back so Isla and Sai could see what she saw.

The holes lined up perfectly over a *T*, an *E*, an *L*, another *E*, a *P*, an *H*, an *O*, an *N*, and another *E*.

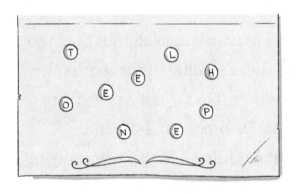

"Telephone," Isla said with amazement.

"I told you those holes were important," Sai said, raising his hand for a high five.

Marly slapped it. "On to the next puzzle," she said.

Chapter 6

TELEPHONE

"So, who are we supposed to call? And what's their number?" Sai asked.

Marly had no idea. She stared at the ink drawing at the top of the paper. There was a phone on the desk in the drawing. But no phone number.

"I guess that's the next thing we have to figure out," Isla said.

Marly slipped the paper back inside their notebook, then they went into the library.

Sai nudged Marly. "Better put your patch

back over your eye," he whispered. "You don't want to get in trouble with your mom."

Marly quickly slid her patch back over her eye. "Thanks," she whispered.

They found Marly's mom sitting on a green chair over by the windows. "Done already?" she asked, glancing up from a gardening magazine.

"For now," Marly said. "We have a new clue, but we don't know what it means yet."

Mom closed her magazine and set it on a table beside her. "What's the clue?"

"Telephone," Isla replied.

"We don't know who we're supposed to call," Marly said.

"Or what their number is," Sai added.

"Maybe you're not supposed to call anyone," Mom suggested. "Maybe you're supposed to find a telephone."

Sai threw his hands in the air. "There are a bazillion telephones in the world! If Mr.

Summerling wanted to give us his treasure, why couldn't he just give it to us? Why make us go through all this?"

"He probably thought it would be more fun this way," Marly said.

"Yeah. And it is fun," Isla put in. "Don't you think, Sai?"

Sai shrugged. "I guess. But it's frustrating, too."

Marly couldn't argue with that.

"Why don't I take you all home and you can think about this telephone a little more," Mom said.

On the way home, Marly rode in the back seat between Isla and Sai. At first it was a quiet ride. Then Isla broke the silence. "We made progress today," she said cheerfully.

"Yeah," Marly agreed. "We probably weren't supposed to solve the whole thing in two days."

"But I *wanted* to solve it in two days," Sai

grumbled. "I wanted to solve it in *one* day, really."

Marly hadn't thought about how long all of this might take. She just wanted to keep working on the puzzle. But it was almost lunchtime now.

"Thanks for the ride, Mrs. Deaver," Sai said when Mom pulled into the Rise and Shine parking lot. He hopped out of the car.

"You're welcome," Mom said. She started to drive away, but Sai ran back to the car, waving his arms.

"Wait!" he yelled. Mom rolled down her window.

"There's a telephone right there." Sai pointed at the phone booth next to the dumpster in the parking lot. "Wanna check it out?"

"Can we?" Marly asked her mom. "You don't have to wait. I can walk home."

"I can, too," Isla said quickly.

It was weird how close they all lived to one another. And they didn't know it until they started working on this treasure hunt together.

"Please?" Marly begged.

Mom thought about it for a second. "I suppose," she said. "It's nice to see you excited about something, honey. And I'm glad to see you making new friends."

Marly wrinkled her nose. This wasn't about making new friends. It was about finishing this treasure hunt and hopefully finding enough money to go visit her *old* friend. She got out of the car and followed Sai and Isla over to the phone booth.

"I can't believe you have a phone booth outside your store," Isla said as Marly's mom drove away. "Who uses pay phones anymore?"

"Yeah, does it even work?" Marly asked.

"I don't know." Sai went inside the booth. "But this *has* to be the telephone. Mr. Summerling came to our store a lot. What other telephone could he be talking about?"

The floor of the phone booth was littered with grass and dirt. Cobwebs clung to the corners and the ceiling. And the old push-button pay phone in the corner was dented and scraped.

"Do you see anything that could be a clue?" Isla asked.

"Not really," Marly replied. She reached around Sai and pushed the coin return door.

It was empty.

Sai picked up the receiver and put it to his ear. "I don't hear anything. Maybe the phone doesn't work."

"You probably have to put  money in," Marly said. "It says, 'Deposit twenty-five cents.' Does anyone have a quarter?"

"I do." Isla pulled one out of her pocket and handed it Marly. Marly put it in the slot.

Sai listened again. "Still nothing."

There was a metal cover next to the coin return on the bottom of the pay phone. Sai wiggled it. "Hey, this moves," he said. He tried to wiggle it some more. It slid a little to one side, then got stuck.

Sai squeezed his pinky into the narrow opening. "I think this is where the money goes. I can feel coins in there. And paper. But the paper doesn't feel like a dollar. It feels like . . . maybe another note!"

Marly tried to help Sai remove the cover, but it wouldn't budge.

"Looks like we need a special key to get it all the way off," Marly said. "See." She touched a small keyhole in the middle of the metal cover.

"Or a screwdriver," Sai said. "I'll go see if my dad has one." He squeezed past Marly and went inside the store. He returned a few minutes later.

"Let's see if this works," he said, wedging the screwdriver into the keyhole. He wiggled it from side to side until the whole cover popped off, revealing a small compartment inside the pay phone.

A few coins and a small metal key fell to the

ground. Marly picked them up. "Where did this come from?" she asked, gazing at the key. "Does it fit the keyhole?" She squinted.

"I don't think so," Sai said. "That little key was in with the coins." There were still a few more coins in the compartment. Along with a folded-up piece of paper.

Sai grabbed the paper and unfolded it while Marly shoved the key inside her pocket.

"It's another paper 'from the desk of Harry P. Summerling,'" Sai said. "But this one makes even less sense than the last one."

Sai was right. There were no letters in this code. It was just a bunch of strange symbols.

"How are we supposed to decode that?" Marly asked.

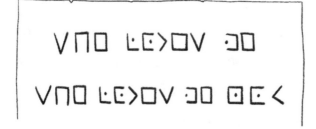

Chapter 7

"**I** know what it is," Isla said, jumping up and down. She was so excited that her cat ears fell off. She caught them before they hit the ground.

"You can read that?" Sai asked.

Marly was as surprised as Sai was. She didn't see how those symbols made any sense at all.

"Well, I can't read it *yet*," Isla said, plopping her cat ears back on her head. "But I know what the code is. Can I please have the notebook?" She held out her hand.

Marly gave her the notebook and they all sat down on the curb. Marly and Sai watched Isla draw a tic-tac-toe grid.

"Tic-tac-toe?" Sai looked confused.

"No. Well, sort of," Isla said thoughtfully. "It's a pigpen code. I'll show you how it works." Instead of X's or O's, Isla put an *A*, a *B*, and a *C* in the top three squares of the tic-tac-toe grid. Then *D*, *E*, and *F* in the middle squares, and *G*, *H*, and *I* in the bottom squares. "Mr. Summerling taught it to me last year and we used it to write some of our letters to each other."

She drew another tic-tac-toe grid beside the first grid and wrote *J*, *K*, *L*, *M*, *N*, *O*, *P*, *Q*, and *R* in those boxes. But this time she added a dot to each of the nine boxes.

"What are the dots for?" Sai asked.

"I'll show you when I'm done," Isla said. She drew two large X's below the tic-tac-toe grids. Then, beginning at the top of the first X, she wrote *S*, *T*, *U*, and *V* in each space where the lines of the X crossed. And *W*, *X*, *Y*, and *Z* in the spaces where the lines of the second X crossed. Finally, she added dots to all the letters in the second X.

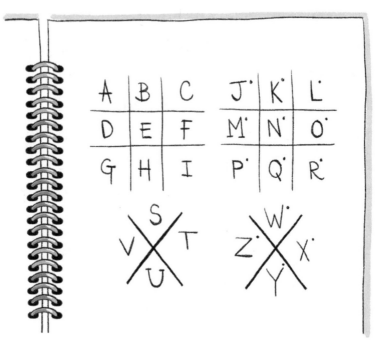

Marly and Sai shrugged at each other. Neither of them had any idea what Isla's drawings had to do with Mr. Summerling's code.

"Okay, look at the first symbol in the code," Isla said.

"It's a V," Marly said. She still didn't get it.

Isla touched her pencil to the *S* she drew inside the first X. The one without the dots. "See?" She traced the lines around the *S*. They formed a V. Like the symbol on the paper. She wrote *S* below the V symbol.

The next symbol sort of looked like an *N*. Marly pointed at the bottom middle square on the first tic-tac-toe grid. "Is the next letter an *H*?"

"Uh-huh." Isla wrote *H* below the second symbol.

"Ohhh, I get it," Sai said. "We have to match the symbols on the paper to the lines of the tic-tac-toe grids or the X's, and then fill in the right letter."

"Yes. We also have to pay attention to whether there's a dot in the symbol. That's how we tell which tic-tac-toe board and which X to use," Isla explained.

Sai skipped ahead to the second word of the code. "This one that looks like an L with a dot inside of it really *is* an L. Right? Because it says so right here." He pointed to the *L* inside Isla's second tic-tac-toe grid.

"Right," Isla said. She wrote an *L* below that symbol on the paper.

"And the next one is an *O*," Marly said, matching the *C* with the dot inside to the *O* in Isla's second tic-tac-toe grid.

"I can't believe you and Mr. Summerling wrote whole letters to each other like this," Sai said.

Neither could Marly. What a lot of work!

Isla grinned. "It was fun."

"Let me solve part of the code," Sai said.

"We should all solve part of it," Marly said. She watched Sai write:

SHELOVESME

"Okay. You can do the rest." Sai handed the notebook and pencil to Marly.

There wasn't much left to figure out. The first three "words" on the second line were the same as the first three words on the top line:

SHELOVESME

And Marly was pretty sure she knew what

the final word was. But she double-checked each letter to make sure she was right.

N O T

"'She loves me, she loves me not,'" Marly read out loud.

"Great," Sai said. "Another puzzle to solve."

Chapter 8

SHE LOVES ME, SHE LOVES ME NOT

"Well, obviously this one has something to do with flowers," Isla said, stretching her legs out in front of her. Marly nodded in agreement.

"What do you mean 'obviously'?" Sai asked.

"Haven't you ever played 'he loves me, he loves me not'?" Marly asked.

Sai looked confused.

"You know. You take a flower—" Marly started to explain, but Sai still looked blank. "Usually it's a daisy with white petals and a

75

yellow center. You pull off one of the petals and say, 'He loves me.' Then you pull off another petal and say, 'He loves me not.'" Marly pretended to pluck petals from an imaginary daisy in her hand. "You keep doing that until you only have one petal left."

"Then what?" Sai asked.

"Then you know whether the person loves you or not," Isla said.

Sai scrunched up his face. "That's weird," he said. "Plus, that's not what the code says. It says *she* loves me, not *he* loves me." He waved the paper in the girls' faces. "Maybe the code is about Mrs. Summerling."

"I don't think there is a Mrs. Summerling," Marly said. She didn't remember a lady ever living next door.

"There must've been one once. Otherwise where did Jay Summerling come from?" Sai said.

"I think the puzzle is about daisies," Isla said.

"Well, there's a flower shop over there." Sai pointed across the street to a building with several stores. "They probably have daisies. We could see if there's a clue in any of them."

"Okay." Marly stood up. From this distance, she couldn't read any of the signs above the stores, not even when she squinted or moved her patch. But if Sai said one of those stores was a flower shop, then she believed him.

Sai went to tell his dad where they were going, then they walked across the street.

Marly opened the door to Beautiful Blossoms and felt like she was walking into a garden. There were flowers everywhere. Her mom would love this store. Over by the cash register, water trickled into an indoor pond.

"Can I help you?" a lady with a high ponytail asked. She was arranging flowers in a vase at a huge counter.

"We'd like to see some daisies, please," Marly said.

"Sure. How many would you like?"

"Oh, we don't want to buy them. We just want to look at them," Sai said.

The lady gave them a curious glance. "They're over here," she said, leading the way to a glass case. Her ponytail swished from side to side.

Marly, Isla, and Sai stared at several large bouquets behind the glass.

"Anybody see any clues?" Marly asked.

"Clues?" the lady said, stepping closer.

"Did you know Mr. Summerling?" Isla asked.

"The guy with the metal detector? Sure, everyone knows him." The lady smiled.

"Did he ever come in here?" Marly asked.

"Did he, by any chance, leave any clues for us in those daisies?" Sai asked.

"I don't think so," the lady said. "These daisies were freshly cut this morning."

"So much for that idea," Sai said as they left the store. "I'm hungry. Let's go to my house. My mom will make us lunch."

Marly took a bite of—she'd already forgotten what Sai's mom called the mashed-potato-filled crepe on her plate. "What is this again?" she asked Sai's mom as she chewed.

"It's called dosa. Do you like it?" Sai's mom asked.

Marly nodded eagerly. "It's really good."

Sai's mom looked pleased. "How is the treasure hunt coming?" she asked.

"Fine," Marly and Isla said at the same time.

"Slow," Sai said.

"Oh, come on. It's not going that slow." Marly took another bite of the delicious dosa. She couldn't imagine her mom or Aubrey's mom making anything like this. Marly's mom usually made sandwiches for lunch. And Aubrey's mom made macaroni and cheese.

"We're doing good," Isla told Sai's mom. "First, we unscrambled words to solve the first code. Then we found a clue hidden on the *Little Bear* statue outside the library. I liked that one, by the way."

"Me too," Marly said. "That clue led us to the phone booth outside your store, where we found the pigpen puzzle. And now we have to do something with daisies."

But what?

"You'll figure it out," Sai's mom said. "I can't wait to see what you find when you get to the end of the treasure hunt."

"Neither can we," Marly said.

"I still wish Mr. Summerling had just given us whatever he wanted to give us," Sai grumbled.

"I'm glad he didn't," Sai's mom said as she started clearing the table. "You appreciate things that you have to work for."

Marly carried her dishes to the sink. The

words *she loves me, she loves me not* rolled around inside her head. "Maybe it's not about daisies," she said to Sai and Isla. "Maybe it's a poem. Or a song."

"Let's google it," Sai suggested. There was a laptop on a small desk behind the sink.

Marly and Isla gathered around while Sai opened the laptop and typed "she loves me she loves me not" into the search bar. He clicked on the first result and read out loud, "It's a fortune-telling game of French origin . . . played by plucking the petals from a flower."

"Not just any flower. Daisies," Isla said.

Marly suddenly remembered something. "Hey, weren't there daisies in front of Mr. Summerling's house? Like, lots of them?"

"Yes, there were!" Isla's eyes shined with excitement. But then her face fell. "We can't get in there. There's a lock on the gate, remember?"

"Well, look what else we found in that pay phone besides the 'she loves me, she loves me not' clue." Marly reached into her pocket and pulled out the tiny key.

DANGEROUS DAISIES

The weeds in Mr. Summerling's yard were taller today than they'd been the day before. And it almost seemed like there was more junk scattered around the yard, but maybe that was Marly's imagination.

Marly wiggled the key into the padlock on the gate. "It fits!" She turned the key with one hand and pulled on the padlock with the other.

"Aha!" Sai cried as the lock snapped open.

Marly removed the padlock and opened

the gate, then they all walked into Mr. Summerling's overgrown yard.

"Look at all the daisies," Marly said. There were more than she'd remembered. There were patches of them up by the house and all around the big oak tree in the front yard.

"Yeah, they're—" Isla froze. The color

drained from her face. "Uh-oh. I shouldn't be here," she said, backing up slowly.

"What do you mean?" Marly squinted at her.

"Bees," she said, barely above a whisper.

"Ack!" Sai leaped backward. "I don't like bees, either. And you're right. Those flowers are covered with them!"

Marly rolled her eyes. "I see *two* bees. And they won't bother you if you don't bother them. Come on. They're just trying to get pollen."

"No, you don't understand," Isla said. "I'm allergic. See?" She raised her arm so Marly and Sai could read her bracelet. It said BEE STING ALLERGY. "And my mom has my EpiPen."

"Oh," Marly said, suddenly worried. What would they do if Isla got stung?

"It's okay. You guys go look. I'll wait here," Isla said. She backed all the way to the gate.

"Are you sure?" Marly said, biting her lip.

Isla nodded. "We need to find out if there's anything hidden in those daisies."

But Sai still hesitated. "Are you sure the bees won't bother us?" he asked Marly.

"Pretty sure," she said. They needed to complete this treasure hunt. And if Isla couldn't go near the flowers, then Marly and Sai would have to.

"Come on." Marly marched over to the closest patch of daisies with more confidence than she felt. She bent down and felt around under the leaves. She didn't feel anything unusual.

Sai walked slowly to another patch of daisies. "Hey, there's a gap in the flowers here," he said, dropping to his knees. "And the dirt is chunky. Like someone's been digging in it."

Marly went to see. "Then maybe we should dig there, too," she said.

Marly and Sai tried to dig with their hands, but it was hard without a shovel. And even with all the junk, there didn't seem to be a single shovel in Mr. Summerling's yard.

"Hey, Isla," Marly called. "Can you go over to my house and ask my mom for a shovel?"

"Get two!" Sai said.

"I don't know," Isla said nervously. "I thought you guys were just going to look around the daisies. Do you really think it's a good idea to dig in Mr. Summerling's flowers?"

"If he didn't want us to dig, he should've told us where the treasure is," Sai said. "It could be right here." He patted the ground in front of him.

"Well . . . okay," Isla said. She ran over to Marly's house and came back a few minutes later with two hand shovels.

The bees hadn't bothered anyone yet. Marly and Sai started digging while Isla watched from the gate.

"Hmm," Sai said when they had a hole that was about four inches deep. "Maybe we were wrong. What if there isn't anything in here?"

"Keep digging," Marly said. A few minutes later, she sat back on her heels. "I have another idea. Isla, could you go ask my mom for my old metal detector? Mr. Summerling gave it to me a couple years ago. That'll tell us whether or not there's anything under here."

"Only if it's metal," Sai pointed out.

"True," Marly said. Maybe that wasn't such a great idea after all.

"I don't know," Isla said. "Mr. Summerling loved metal detectors. If he buried something, I'd bet it's metal." She ran next door again. While she was gone, Marly and Sai continued digging.

"Here you go," Isla called from the sidewalk when she returned with the metal detector. "Your mom put fresh batteries in it, too."

Marly ran to get it. "Great! Thanks," she said. It had been a while since she'd used her metal detector. She hoped she remembered how it worked. She found the on/off switch and turned it on. It let out a low hum.

Marly moved it slowly around the daisies by the tree. The hum didn't change.

"Bring it over here," Sai said, rising up on his knees.

The hum of the metal detector remained constant as Marly walked it across the grass. But as soon as she brought it near the hole she and Sai had dug, it started beeping loud and fast.

"There *is* something here!" Sai exclaimed. He dug harder. Faster.

Marly laid the metal detector down and picked up the other shovel so she could help dig. Dirt flew everywhere.

Finally, Sai's shovel struck something hard. "We found the treasure!" he cried.

"The *actual* treasure?" Isla called, leaning toward them.

"We don't know yet," Marly called back. She and Sai brushed the dirt off the top of an old metal box. They tried to pull it out of the hole, but they couldn't get a good hold on it.

"We have to dig more around it to get it out," Marly said.

"What is it? What is it?" Isla called, bouncing from one foot to the other.

Marly and Sai dug a little trench all around the box, then Sai pulled it from the hole. It was about the size and shape of Marly's pencil case. And it was covered in so much dirt that Marly couldn't tell whether the box was gray or blue. Two rusty clips held it closed.

"How much money do you think is in here?" Sai rubbed his hands together.

"I don't know," Marly said. "But we should all open it together." She picked up the box and carried it over to Isla.

They all sat down on the sidewalk with the box between them. Isla's headband cast a cat ear shadow over the box.

"You open it," Marly said to Isla. "It's only fair, since you didn't get to help us dig it out."

Isla took a deep breath, released the clips, and opened the box.

They all groaned.

All that was inside was another folded piece of paper.

Chapter 10

CODE
1-5-3

"ARGH!" Sai flopped back onto the grass. "How many puzzles are we doing to have to solve before we finally get the treasure?"

Marly was wondering the same thing. She was so sure the metal box was going to be full of treasure. So sure the hunt was over.

Would it *ever* be over?

"Well, let's see what this one says." Isla grabbed the paper and unfolded it. It was the same stationery from Harry Summerling. It read:

From the Desk of Harry P. Summerling

41.8037N 91.5710W

Code 1 - 5 - 3

"What kind of puzzle is that?" Marly asked.

"No idea," Isla said, staring at the paper in her hand. She didn't seem as frustrated as Sai and Marly were. "Maybe for the first part, we have to change the numbers into letters and the letters into numbers," she suggested. "Like 4 would be *D* because it's the fourth letter of the alphabet."

Marly took a deep breath and opened their notebook. "Let's see if that works," she said as she wrote *D A*.

"The next letter is an *H*," Sai said. Marly wrote that down, too.

"What do we do with the zero?" Isla asked.

"Maybe the zero is really an *O* and we're supposed to change it into a number," Sai said. He counted on his fingers while mouthing the alphabet to himself. "*O* is the fifteenth letter of the alphabet."

Isla and Sai helped Marly translate the whole top line. They ended up with:

D A. H 15 C G 14 I A. E G A 15 23

"That doesn't make any sense," Marly said.

"Maybe the top numbers are library book numbers," Sai said.

Isla raised an eyebrow. "You mean Dewey decimal numbers?"

"I don't think so," Marly said. "Dewey decimal numbers have three numbers, then a period, then more numbers. Like 305.4567."

Marly remembered that from their library unit at school.

"Okay, let's work on the bottom part," Isla said. "Code 1-5-3. What could that be?"

They looked at each another blankly.

"Maybe we should sleep on it," Isla said. "Can you guys come over to my house tomorrow morning and work on this puzzle then?"

"I have summer school tomorrow morning," Sai said. "But I could come in the afternoon."

"I'm free tomorrow afternoon," Marly said.

"See you tomorrow," Isla said.

When Marly returned home, she found her mom weeding her garden. "How're the puzzles coming along?" Mom asked.

Marly shrugged.

Mom gave Marly a curious look. "What's the matter, honey?"

"I thought we found the treasure buried in Mr. Summerling's yard. But it turned out to be another puzzle," Marly said.

"So?" Mom added a handful of weeds to the pile beside her. "Why the long face?"

"Well . . ." Marly felt bad about what she was about to say. "What if there isn't any treasure? A lot of people think Mr. Summerling was a silly old man. His own son says there's no treasure. What if Isla, Sai, and I go from puzzle to puzzle for the rest of the summer and we never find any treasure?"

"Would that be so bad?" Mom asked.

Marly thought that was a weird thing for her mother to say.

"What did Mr. Summerling say that time you asked him if he ever found any treasure?" Mom tossed more weeds onto the pile. "'Not all treasure is silver and gold'?"

Marly rubbed her unpatched eye. What did that even mean?

"Seems to me you've already found some treasure," Mom said.

Marly clucked her tongue. "No, we haven't," she said. "We just keep finding new puzzles!"

"But you've made some new friends in the process," Mom said, cupping Marly's cheek in her hand.

Had she? Marly wondered.

She liked Isla and Sai. She liked how careful and thoughtful Isla was, and even though Sai was kind of impatient, he was funny. He wasn't

99

funny in the same way Aubrey was, but he made Marly and Isla laugh.

Still, Marly couldn't imagine playing "let's pretend we're . . ." with either Sai or Isla.

"I know you miss Aubrey a lot." Mom went to get the hose. "But in time, I think Isla and Sai could turn out to be as good of friends to you as Aubrey was."

"Really?" Marly asked.

"Well, that's up to you," Mom said. "Friendship is kind of like a garden. If you water it, it grows. If you don't . . ." Mom turned on the hose.

It had been a whole day since Marly last checked for an email from Aubrey. There probably wouldn't be one today either, but Marly went into the house to check anyway. Just in case.

She found the family iPad on the kitchen counter. She turned it on and touched her email app. She almost dropped the iPad in shock when she saw she had an email! She sat down to read it.

From: Aubrey Etoh
To: Marly Deaver
Subject: Sorry!
Hi Marly,
I'm so, so sorry I haven't written. You know I don't really like writing.

Marly smiled. Yeah, she knew that about Aubrey. Marly had always wanted the two of them to write out their best "let's pretend we're . . ." skits as short stories, but Aubrey never wanted to. Because she hated writing.

I've also been really, really busy. My mom signed me up for softball! 🙁 I didn't want to do it at first, but guess what? It turns out I like softball! 🏏 ♡

Softball! Marly thought. She couldn't imagine Aubrey playing softball.

Or was it *herself* she couldn't imagine playing softball? Her amblyopia made catching and hitting a ball in gym pretty hard.

That's really, really cool that your neighbor left you and Isla and Sai some treasure. Solving puzzles sounds kind of boring. But I hope you find enough treasure to buy a plane ticket and come visit me. I miss playing "let's pretend we're . . ." with you. I tried to play it with my new softball friends, but they aren't as good at it as you are.
Best Friends 4-Ever,
Aubrey

Marly leaned back in her chair. All along she'd been wishing she was doing this treasure hunt with Aubrey instead of Isla and Sai. But it hadn't occurred to her until just now that Aubrey probably wouldn't have enjoyed the puzzles as much as Isla and Sai did. How did she not know that?

Maybe it was good she was doing this with Isla and Sai after all.

"We have to stay outside," Isla told Marly and Sai the next afternoon. "Liam is taking a nap."

"That's okay," Marly said. Isla had the most amazing play structure in her backyard. It had two slides, a climbing wall, monkey bars, a clubhouse, and a picnic table.

Sai raced over to it. He jumped and grabbed the first monkey bar, then kicked his legs up so he could hang upside down. Marly and Isla went over to the little picnic table under one of the slides and took out the paper with the latest puzzle.

"This seems like an extra hard puzzle,"
Marly said, scratching her head.

Isla adjusted her green cat ears. "I think so,
too," she said.

They studied the paper.

"You could come over here and help us, you know," Marly told Sai.

"I'm helping," Sai said. "I think better when I'm upside down."

Marly sighed. She glanced around the yard. A flat rooster that was perched at the top of a weather vane caught her eye. The rooster danced between the *N* and the *W*.

"Hey," Marly said, squinting at the rooster. "The *N* and *W* could be directions. Maybe this puzzle has something to do with numbers on a compass."

"I don't think there are numbers on a compass," Isla said.

Sai swung his legs backward over his head and jumped down. "Told you being upside down helps me think," he said, walking over to them. "Because guess what? I know what we need to do to solve the puzzle!"

Chapter 11

INTO THE WOODS

"What do we need to do?" Marly asked Sai.

"We need to go geocaching!" he replied.

Marly and Isla looked at each other blankly.

"What? Haven't you guys ever been geocaching?" Sai asked.

"I don't even know what that is," Isla said, tossing her hair over her shoulder.

"It's sort of a treasure hunt," Sai said.

"But we're already on a treasure hunt," Marly said.

"So, a treasure hunt within a treasure hunt?" Isla asked.

"Sort of," Sai said. "I can't believe you guys don't know about geocaching. It's really fun! There are geocaches hidden all over the world and you use your GPS to find them." He pointed at the top numbers on the clue. "Those could be latitude and longitude numbers. Does anyone have a GPS? We could type them in and find out."

"You mean a cell phone?" Isla asked.

"No, I mean a GPS. But a cell phone would work, too, if you have one. Do either of you?" Sai asked.

Marly shook her head. "I'm not allowed to get one until middle school."

"Me either," Isla said.

"Then let's go over to my house and get my GPS," Sai said.

Sai's GPS was about the size of a deck of cards. It was yellow and black, with rubber around the edges. The screen was black and white.

"It's pretty old, but it works," Sai said. He pushed some buttons, then typed in 41.8037N and 91.5710W. An arrow spun on the screen, then stopped.

"See?" Sai said. "It is latitude and longitude. We're about a mile away from 41.8037N and 91.5710W." He started walking in the direction the GPS told him to walk.

Marly hurried along beside him. "Okay, so what is Code 1-5-3 then?" Isla asked.

"I don't know," Sai said with a shrug. "Let's find 41.8037N and 91.5710W first. Then we can worry about Code 1-5-3."

Sai's GPS led them back to Marly's street. They walked past Marly's house, past Mr. Summerling's house, and around the corner to the dead end at the edge of the woods.

"We still have another half mile to go," Sai said, charging into the woods. There was no trail. Just trees and underbrush. A bed of pine needles covered the ground.

"Wait," Isla said. She pointed at a sign that said Private Property.

"Whose property is it?" Marly asked, looking around.

"Could it be Mr. Summerling's?" Sai asked.

"Maybe," Marly said.

"I don't know." Isla twisted her hair. "I don't know if we should go wandering around in there."

"Oh, I think we should," Sai said, clutching the GPS in his hand. "We're on the right track. And it's not far."

Marly reached for Isla's hand. "Come on. It's only half a mile. And it's probably Mr. Summerling's property, so it's okay." *Probably*.

Isla still didn't budge.

"You want to find the treasure, don't you?" Sai asked.

"Yeah," Isla admitted. She took Marly's hand and they continued deeper into the woods.

It was quiet in there. So quiet. And the tall pine trees made it feel darker than it actually was.

"What if we get lost?" Isla worried as they meandered around one tree after another.

"We won't. Not when we have a GPS," Sai said. "But . . ." He stopped walking and stared at the gadget in his hand. "Sometimes it's hard to get a good signal when you're in the woods."

"What?" Isla cried.

"It's fine," Marly said. "These woods aren't that big. Let's keep going."

The farther they walked, the more Marly began to wonder if they were walking around in circles. But she didn't want to scare Isla by saying that out loud.

"Whatever we're looking for isn't far," Sai said.

The trees were getting thicker. Somewhere in the distance a twig snapped.

Sai slowed his pace. "It should be right around here," he said, looking from side to side.

Marly was the first to see it. She squealed

with delight. "There." She pointed up into the trees.

"I don't know what you're pointing at," Isla said.

"Me either," Sai said.

"Right there." Marly pointed again. It wasn't easy to spot. The leaves on the trees around it hid it pretty well. But if you stood in the exact right spot, even with an eye patch, you could see the small wooden house nestled in the branches of a sturdy tree.

"A tree house?" Isla said.

Sai grinned. "That must be it," he said. "We're very close to 41.8037N and 91.5710W." He held the GPS so Marly and Isla could see it, but they were already running toward the tree.

"Wait for me!" Sai cried, hurrying after them."How do we get up there?" Marly craned her neck. They walked slowly around the tree and discovered a rope ladder hanging from a platform outside the little wooden house.

"Are you sure that's sturdy?" Isla asked as Marly put her foot on the bottom rung.

"Pretty sure," Marly said. She started climbing. When she reached the top, she hoisted herself up onto a small landing outside the tree house.

There was a kid-size door with a lock on it. But the lock didn't require a key. It required three numbers. And Marly knew exactly which numbers to try.

Chapter 12

THE TREASURE TROOP

Marly spun the dials on the lock to 1-5-3. The lock clicked open.

"Come on up!" Marly called down to Isla and Sai. She opened the small door and crawled inside the tree house. Once inside, she could stand all the way up.

"Wow. This is so cool," Sai said, crawling in behind Marly. Isla was right on his heels.

The tree house had a wooden roof, windows with real glass, and plain red curtains that matched a red rug in the middle of the floor. Three stools cut from tree stumps circled a small table. And there was another paper on the table, with the usual words *From the Desk of Harry P. Summerling* at the top.

From the Desk of Harry P. Summerling

congratulations to My treAsure troop! you've worKed hard and now you've come to the End of this treasure hunt. i suppose you're wondering what your prize is. it's this clubhouse! come here Anytime to unwind, play a game, and enjoy each other's company. you've each, in your own way, been a good friend To me. now please be good friends to one another. when good friends are around, anything can happen!

—harry p. summerling

"What? He's giving us a tree house?" Sai cried.

"Wow," Isla said.

There was a small shelf with board games (including Monopoly!) against one wall. And crudely drawn pictures on all four walls. The one across from Marly was a teddy bear. The one behind her was a globe. The one to her right was a telephone. And the one to her left was a vase of flowers.

"Now we know why Mr. Summerling left his treasure to us instead of to his son," Marly said. "I don't think Jay Summerling would want a tree house."

Sai laughed. "Can you imagine him climbing up here in that fancy suit?"

"No way." Isla shook her head. Her smile froze as she glanced down at the paper from the table. She picked it up.

"You know . . . ," Isla said, reading the paper again, "there's something weird about this note. Some of the words that should be capitalized aren't. But then there are random capital letters in other places."

Marly leaned over. "Yeah, you're right."

"Maybe the treasure hunt isn't really over," Sai said, rubbing his hands together.

"Do the capital letters spell anything?" Marly asked.

"Maket?" Sai said.

"I think you missed an *A*," Isla said. "Let's go in order. *M . . . A . . . K . . . E . . . A . . . T*."

"That's still not a word," Marly said.

"But it's got a word in it," Sai said. "*E, A, T*. That spells *eat*."

"Two words," Isla said. "Make and at. And that uses all the letters." She set the paper back on the table.

Marly reached into her bag and pulled out their notebook. "Maybe the letters are scrambled, and we have to unscramble them."

Tame? Meat? Make? She made a list in the

notebook. But no matter what Marly tried to spell, there were always letters left over.

Except when she spelled *make* and *at*.

She tried separating the *A* and the *T*. "Make a T?" she said. She drew a large *T*. But that didn't help.

She laid her pencil down and watched it roll across the table.

"There's something weird about the pictures on the walls, too," Isla said, glancing all around. "They look like a little kid drew them."

"The telephone one is definitely weird," Sai said. "Who paints a picture of a telephone and hangs it on the wall?"

"Wait. Bear, telephone, flowers—" Isla began.

"Not just flowers. Daisies!" Marly leaped to her feet. "Except for the globe, they're all part of the puzzles we solved."

"So is the globe," Sai said. He got up, too.

"Globes have longitude and latitude. That's how we found this place."

"See how all the pictures are across from each other?" Marly pointed. "The bear is across from the globe and the daisies are across from the phone. What if we drew imaginary lines from each picture to the picture across from it?"

"We'd have a *T*," Isla said.

Sai walked over. "The *T* should be . . ." He lined himself up with the pictures and held his arms out. "Right here." He looked down at the red rug beneath his feet.

"I say we roll up that rug," Marly said, dropping to her knees. Sai hopped off the rug, and together he, Marly and Isla rolled it up. But all that was under there was a scuffed wood floor.

Marly and Isla tapped on the boards. One made a hollow sound when Marly tapped on it. She pulled on the edges, and it came right up.

"There's something in there," Isla said, reaching inside the hole. Whatever it was was too big to fit through the opening.

Sai pulled on the next board. That one came up, too. And so did the board next to that one.

A secret compartment! Inside, nestled at the bottom, was a blue metal box. It looked a lot like the box they'd found buried in Mr. Summerling's yard, except this one could have been brand-new. Marly and Sai unclipped the top. And Isla opened the lid.

The box contained several more papers, all marked with *From the Desk of Harry P. Summerling*. The top one said:

A place to hide all your treasure.

But the others were blank.

"Cool!" Marly grinned. "Every clubhouse needs a secret hiding spot."

"But we don't have any treasure to hide in

there," Sai said, disappointed.

"I've got a silver dollar at home," Isla said, flipping her hair over her shoulder. She frowned. "My brother Gavin has already tried to steal it twice. Maybe I'll hide it in there."

That gave Sai an idea. "I've got some coins from India that I could hide in there."

Marly didn't have anything like that to put in the treasure chest. But if she really was able to stop wearing her eye patches in a few weeks, maybe she'd put those in there. She couldn't really explain why that felt like a good idea. It just did.

"I wish we could tell Mr. Summerling that we solved his treasure hunt," Marly said when they closed up the secret compartment.

"I think he knows," Isla said.

"Yeah," Sai agreed.

Maybe, Marly thought to herself. Either way, it was pretty great of him to bring her, Isla, and Sai together. It was like he knew how badly she missed Aubrey and so he gave her the thing she needed most. Not money for a plane ticket to go visit her old friend, but new friends to hang out with right here in Sandford.

"I have a feeling we're going to have lots of adventures together in this tree house," Isla said.

"I think so, too," Marly said.

"Here's to adventure!" Sai said as he extended his hand palm down.

Isla put her hand on top of Sai's. Marly put her hand on top of Isla's. And together, they raised their clasped hands. Marly couldn't wait for their next adventure to begin.

THE END